P9-DEY-312

Dear Parent:
Your child's love of reading starts here!

Every child learns to read in a different way and at his or her own speed. Some go back and forth between reading levels and read favorite books again and again. Others read through each level in order. You can help your young reader improve and become more confident by encouraging his or her own interests and abilities. From books your child reads with you to the first books he or she reads alone, there are I Can Read Books for every stage of reading:

SHARED READING
Basic language, word repetition, and whimsical illustrations, ideal for sharing with your emergent reader

BEGINNING READING
Short sentences, familiar words, and simple concepts for children eager to read on their own

READING WITH HELP
Engaging stories, longer sentences, and language play for developing readers

READING ALONE
Complex plots, challenging vocabulary, and high-interest topics for the independent reader

ADVANCED READING
Short paragraphs, chapters, and exciting themes for the perfect bridge to chapter books

I Can Read Books have introduced children to the joy of reading since 1957. Featuring award-winning authors and illustrators and a fabulous cast of beloved characters, I Can Read Books set the standard for beginning readers.

A lifetime of discovery begins with the magical words "I Can Read!"

Visit www.icanread.com for information
on enriching your child's reading experience.

For Grace.
And the tales you're going to tell.
—R.S.

I Can Read Book® is a trademark of HarperCollins Publishers.

Splat the Cat: A Whale of a Tale
Copyright © 2013 by Rob Scotton
All rights reserved. Manufactured in China.
No part of this book may be used or reproduced in any manner whatsoever without written permission except in the case of brief
quotations embodied in critical articles and reviews. For information address HarperCollins Children's Books, a division of
HarperCollins Publishers, 10 East 53rd Street, New York, NY 10022.
www.icanread.com

Library of Congress catalog card number: 2012949618
ISBN 978-0-06-209024-9 (trade bdg.) —ISBN 978-0-06-209022-5 (pbk.)

13 14 15 16 17 SCP 10 9 8 7 6 5 4 3 2 1

❖

First Edition

I Can Read!

BEGINNING
1
READING

Splat the Cat
A Whale of a Tale

Based on the bestselling books
by **Rob Scotton**

Cover art by Rick Farley

Text by Amy Hsu Lin

Interior illustrations by Robert Eberz

HARPER
An Imprint of HarperCollinsPublishers

Splat the Cat buckled his seat belt.

"Let's go!" he yelled.

"It's vacation time!"

Everyone else piled in.

"Bring me back a shell so I can hear the sea, too!" said Grandpa.

"When I come back,

I'll have a shell to show

and a story to tell," Splat said.

Grandpa waved farewell.

"Hello, beach!" said Splat.

Splat's toes wiggled

in the soft sand.

Now he could look for a shell.

Dad said, "Splat, will you please

help me with the umbrella?"

"Okay," Splat said.

"Then I'm going to find a shell."

"Splat, first help me spell!"

begged Little Sis.

"Okay," Splat said.

"After that,

I have to look for a shell."

my Castl

GRRRR

Just then Splat's tummy

made a rumble.

"Time for ice cream and fish,"
Splat said.

"Then shell hunting!"

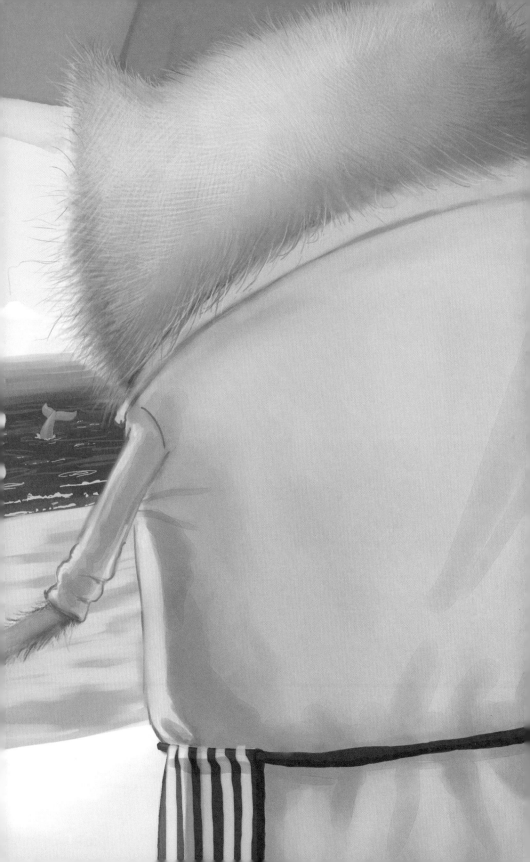

Splat began his search.

He wanted to bring home

the sound of the sea for Grandpa.

First Splat found

a dull snail shell.

It was way too small.

Then Splat found

a frail eggshell.

That was the wrong kind of shell,

and it had a funny smell.

Splat thought he saw a pale shell
buried in the sand.

17

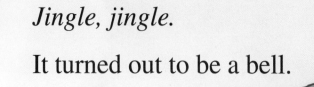

Jingle, jingle.

It turned out to be a bell.

Almost all the other shells

that Splat saw were broken.

"How odd," said Splat.

"What can I do?

I have no shell for show-and-tell.

I have no shell for Grandpa."

Splat took his pail
and walked along the water.
He followed the trail
of broken shells.

Then Splat heard a *crack*!

A shell fell.

The shell broke.

Splat looked up.

A gull was dropping shells
all over the shore.

Splat ran after the gull.

He tried to catch the shells

before they fell.

Splat ran back and forth and then . . .

splat!

He fell into a swell!

Splat flailed about.

Then . . . *thump*.

He landed on something.

Something BIG!

It was a whale!

"Can you help me

catch a shell?"

Splat asked.

The whale spouted.

Sploosh!

Water went up.

Splat went up, too.

The gull dropped another shell,

and Splat caught it.

Whoosh!

The whale stopped spouting.

Splat slid down the whale's tail
and onto the sandy shore.

Splat shook the water out of his ears

and held up the shell.

He heard the roaring swell!

All's well that ends well,

Splat thought happily.

On the way home,

Splat thought about

the whale of a tale

he would tell to Grandpa.

Then he fell asleep

listening to the sound of the sea.